Everybody Wins!

by Sheila Bruce
Illustrated by Paige Billin-Frye

The Kane Press
New York

Book Design/Art Direction: Roberta Pressel

Library of Congress Cataloging-in-Publication Data

Bruce, Sheila.
    Everybody wins!/Sheila Bruce; illustrated by Paige Billin-Frye.
      p. cm. — (Math matters.)
    Summary: When Oscar enters a number of contests he learns to divide both the costs and the rewards with his friends.
    ISBN 1-57565-101-7 (pbk. : alk. paper)
    [1. Division—Fiction. 2. Contests—Fiction. 3. Friendship—Fiction.] I. Billin-Frye,
    Paige, ill. II. Title. III. Series.
    PZ7.B82814 Ev 2000
    [E]—dc21   00-043817
                                                        CIP
                                                           AC

10 9 8 7 6 5 4

First published in the United States of America in 2001 by Kane Press, Inc.
Printed in Hong Kong.

MATH MATTERS is a registered trademark of Kane Press, Inc.

www.kanepress.com

Oscar was eating his favorite lunch, frozen pizza. It was his dog Bob's favorite, too. While he ate, Oscar read about a contest. First prize was 100 frozen pizzas. Oscar got so excited he couldn't swallow.

"Oscar! Are you all right?" asked his
mom.

"I'm fine," he said. "I've just got to enter
this contest!"

Oscar's mother read the contest rules. "You need two Peppy Pooch box tops," she said. "We only have one box."

The deadline for mailing the entry form was the next day. Oscar wondered what to do.

"Take Bob for a walk while you think about it," said his mother.

Oscar and Bob ran into Emmy and her
dog, Newbery. While Bob and Newbery said
hello, Oscar told Emmy about the contest.

"I have a box top," said Emmy. "Newbery
eats Peppy Pooch, too—lots of it."

"We can split the prize if we win," said Oscar. "That's fifty frozen pizzas each!"

"That's a lot of pizza," said Emmy.

They walked to Emmy's house and she gave Oscar a box top. He ran home to fill out the entry form.

$$100 \div 2 = 50$$

While Oscar was mailing his entry form, his friend Hugo rode by.

"What are you mailing?" asked Hugo. Oscar told him about the contest.

"Wish I could enter," said Hugo. "But Tweeter only eats seeds." Tweeter was Hugo's parakeet. He was a quiet bird.

Hugo went home. "I've never won anything," he told Tweeter.

Tweeter just looked at him.

Three weeks later a box appeared on Oscar's porch. He phoned Emmy.

"Guess what?" he said. "We won a prize!"

"Pizza?" asked Emmy.

"Marshmallows," said Oscar. "Twenty-four bags of them. You get twelve."

24 ÷ 2 = 12

"That's a lot of marshmallows," said Emmy.
"Should we take them to the class camp-out?"
    "How many kids in our class?" asked Oscar.
"Twenty-four," said Emmy.
    "A bag for each kid," said Oscar. "Excellent!"

$$24 \div 24 = 1$$

That weekend the class roasted marshmallows around the campfire. They were delicious. Only 20 kids came so there were 4 bags left to share. Everyone thanked Oscar and Emmy.

Hugo said, "You two are so lucky. I've never won anything."

24 ÷ 20 = 1 with 4 left over

A week later at the village fair Oscar saw some people selling raffle tickets. First prize was a giant-screen TV. "Wow," he thought. "It would be so cool to watch baseball on a giant TV! I've just got to enter!"

Save the Giant Pandas
Win a Giant Screen T.V.
Tickets $12

Win Win Win

Each ticket was 12 dollars. Oscar only had 6 dollars. Hugo would have split a ticket with him. But Hugo was away for the weekend.

$$\$12 \div 2 = \$6$$

Oscar called Emmy.

"Six dollars is a lot of money," she said.
"Why don't we split the ticket three ways?
I could pay 4 dollars, you could pay 4 dollars,
and Tony could pay 4 dollars." Tony was
Emmy's new next-door neighbor.

$$\$12 \div 3 = \$4$$

"Fine with me," said Oscar.

"I'll talk to Tony and meet you in five minutes," said Emmy.

When Hugo came back home, Oscar told him about the raffle.

"Wish I'd been here. I could have chipped in," said Hugo. "I've never won anything."

The raffle drawing was two weeks later.
They didn't win a prize. Oscar walked over to
Emmy's house to tell her. Just as he finished,
Hugo rode up.

"Guess what I'm getting for my birthday?"
he said. "Four tickets to the baseball game.
We can all go together!"

Oscar, Hugo, Emmy, and Tony had a great time at the game. Everybody had hot dogs and soda. Tony brought twelve packs of bubble gum with him. He split them.

$12 \div 4 = 3$

Emmy shared a box of caramel corn.
The prize inside was four tiny baseball
cards. Emmy shared them, too.

$$4 \div 4 = 1$$

A few days later Hugo went over to Oscar's house. "There's this contest," he said. "First prize is thirty-six boxes of bubble gum."

"Wow!" said Oscar. He read the entry form. "Are you going to enter?"

"Well…" said Hugo. "I was thinking—maybe you and Emmy could enter with me. You're both pretty lucky."

"We didn't win the raffle," said Oscar.

"You won marshmallows," said Hugo. "I've never won anything."

"Okay," said Oscar. "If we win we'll split the prize three ways."

$$36 \div 3 = 12$$

Oscar and Hugo told Emmy about the contest.

"Twelve boxes," she said. "That's a lot of bubble gum."

"I'll enter with you," said Tony.

"Great!" said Hugo. "Then we can all share the prize."

36 ÷ 4 = 9

As soon as he got home, Hugo filled out the entry form.

"Do you think my luck will change?" Hugo asked Tweeter.

Tweeter pecked him.

A month later Hugo got a letter saying he'd won second prize—a $40 gift certificate to Pet Depot. Oscar, Emmy and Tony came over to celebrate.

"I can't believe it!" said Hugo. "A real prize! And it's better than bubble gum! It's for forty whole dollars!"

"That's a lot of money," said Emmy.

"What's 40 dollars divided four ways?" asked Oscar.

Before anybody else could figure it out, Hugo said, "Ten dollars."

"Perfect" said Tony. "Now I can buy a new cat bed."

$40 \div 4 = \$10$

When they got to Pet Depot, Emmy said, "I'm going to look at chew toys."

"Bob could use some chew toys," said Oscar. "I'll go with you."

Tony headed for the cat department and Hugo took off for the bird section.

A few minutes later Hugo appeared.

"What's in that box?" asked Emmy.

He opened it so they could see inside.
"Cheep!" said a bright blue parakeet.

"A friend for Tweeter," said Hugo. "Think
he'll like her?"

"I think Tweeter's getting the best prize
of all," said Oscar.

And guess what? Tweeter thought so, too!

DIVISION CHART

Here are some ways to divide.

1. Use models.

Split 6 cookies into 3 equal groups.
6 ÷ 3 = 2 cookies in each group

Split 7 cookies into 3 equal grou
7 ÷ 3 = 2 cookies in each group
plus 1 cookie left over

2. Use a related multiplication fact.   21 ÷ 7 = ?

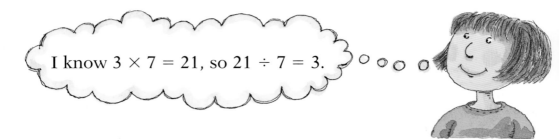

I know 3 × 7 = 21, so 21 ÷ 7 = 3.

3. Find and use patterns.

5 ÷ 5 = 1   18 ÷ 3 = 6

10 ÷ 5 = 2   19 ÷ 3 = 6 plus 1 left over

20 ÷ 5 = 4   20 ÷ 3 = 6 plus 2 left over

40 ÷ 5 = 8   21 ÷ 3 = 7